C000130317

The Edgar Allan Poe of Japan

Some Tales By Edogawa Rampo

With Some Stories Inspired by His Writings

Copyright © 2011 Read Books Ltd.
This book is copyright and may not be
reproduced or copied in any way without
the express permission of the publisher in writing

British Library Cataloguing-in-Publication Data
A catalogue record for this book is available from
the British Library

Contents

The Boy who Drew Cats

LAFCADIO HEARN

A long, long time ago, in a small country village in Japan, there lived a poor farmer and his wife, who were very good people. They had a number of children, and found it hard to feed them all. The elder son was strong enough when only fourteen years old to help his father; and the little girls learned to help their mother almost as soon as they could walk.

But the youngest child, a little boy, did not seem to be fit for hard work. He was very clever – cleverer than all his brothers and sisters; but he was quite weak and small, and people said he could never grow very big. So his parents thought it would be better for him to become a priest than to become a farmer. They took him with them to the village temple one day, and asked the good old priest who lived there if he would have their little boy for his pupil, and teach him all that a priest ought to know.

The old man spoke kindly to the lad, and asked him some hard questions. So clever were the answers that the priest agreed to take the little fellow into the temple as an acolyte, and to educate him for the priesthood.

The boy learned quickly what the old priest taught him, and was very obedient in most things. But he had one fault. He liked to draw cats during study-hours, and to draw cats when cats ought not to have been drawn at all.

Whenever he found himself alone, he drew cats. He drew them on the margins of the priest's books, and on all the screens of the temple, on the walls, and on the pillars. Several times the priest told him this was not right; but he did not stop drawing cats. He drew them because he could not really help it. He had what is called 'the genius of an artist', and just for that reason he was not quite fit to be an acolyte; a good acolyte should study books.

One day after he had drawn some very clever pictures of cats upon a paper screen, the old priest said to him severely, 'My boy, you must go away from this temple at once. You will never make a good priest, but perhaps you will become a great artist. Now let me give you a last piece of advice, and be sure you never forget it. *Avoid large places at night; keep to small!*'

The boy did not know what the priest meant by saying, '*Avoid large places; keep to small!*' He thought and thought, while he was tying up his little bundle of clothes to go away; but he could not understand those words, and he was afraid to speak to the priest any more, except to say good-bye.

He left the temple very sorrowfully, and began to wonder what he should do. If he went straight home he felt his father would punish him for having been disobedient to the priest: so he was afraid to go home. All at once he remembered that at the next village, twelve miles away, there was a very big temple. He had heard there were several priests at that temple; and he made up his mind to go to them and ask them to take him for their acolyte.

Now that big temple was closed up but the boy did not know this fact. The reason it had been closed up was that a goblin had frightened the priests away, and had taken possession of the place. Some brave warriors had afterwards gone to the temple at night to kill the goblin; but they had never been seen alive again. Nobody had ever told these things to the boy; so he walked all the way to the village hoping to be kindly treated by the priests.

When he got to the village it was already dark, and all the people were in bed; but he saw the big temple on a hill on the other end of the principal street, and he saw there was a light in the temple. People who tell the story say the goblin used to make that light, in order to tempt lonely travellers to ask for shelter. The boy went at once to the temple, and knocked. There was no sound inside. He knocked and knocked again; but still nobody came. At last he pushed gently at the door, and was glad to find that it had not been fastened. So he went in and saw a lamp burning - but no priest.

He thought that some priest would be sure to come very soon, and he sat down and waited. Then he noticed that everything in the temple was grey with dust, and thickly spun over with cobwebs. So he thought to himself that the priests would certainly like to have an acolyte, to keep the place clean. He wondered why they had allowed the place to get so dusty. What most pleased him, however, were some big white screens, good to paint cats upon. Though he was tired, he looked at once for a writing box, and found one, and ground some ink, and began to paint cats.

He painted a great many cats upon the screens; and then he began to feel very, very sleepy. He was just on the point of lying down to sleep beside one of the screens, when he suddenly remembered the words: '*Avoid large places – keep to small!*'

The temple was very large; he was alone; and as he thought of these words – though he could not quite understand them – he began to feel for the first time a little afraid; and he resolved to look for a small place in which to sleep. He found a little cabinet, with a sliding door, and went into it and shut himself up. Then he lay down and fell fast asleep.

Very late in the night he was awakened by a most terrible noise – a noise of fighting and screaming. It was so dreadful that he was afraid even to look through a chink of the little cabinet; he lay very still, holding his breath for fright.

The light that had been in the temple went out; but the awful sounds continued, and became more awful, and all the temple shook. After a long time silence came; but the boy was still afraid to move. He did not move until the light of the morning sun shone into the cabinet through the chinks of the little door.

Then he got out of his hiding-place very cautiously, and looked about. The first thing he saw was that all the floor of the temple was covered with blood. And then he saw, lying dead in the middle of it, an enormous monstrous rat – a goblin-rat – bigger than a cow!

But who or what could have killed it? There was no man or other creature to be seen. Suddenly the boy observed that the mouths of all the cats he had drawn the night before were red and wet with blood. Then he knew that the goblin had been killed by the cats which he had drawn. And then also, for the first time, he understood why the wise old priest had said to him: – '*Avoid large places at night; keep to small.*'

Afterwards that boy became a very famous artist. Some of the cats which he drew are still shown to travellers in Japan.

THE HELL OF MIRRORS

by *Edogawa Rampo*

ONE of the queerest friends I ever had was Kan Tanuma. From the very start I suspected that he was mentally unbalanced. Some might have called him just eccentric, but I am convinced he was a lunatic. At any rate, he had one mania – a craze for anything capable of reflecting an image, as well as for all types of lenses. Even as a boy the only toys he would play with were magic lanterns, telescopes, magnifying glasses, kaleidoscopes, prisms, and the like.

Perhaps this strange mania of Tanuma's was hereditary, for his great-grandfather Moribe was also known to have had the same predilection. As evidence there is the collection of objects – primitive glassware and telescopes and ancient books on related subjects – which this Moribe obtained from the early Dutch merchants at Nagasaki. These were handed down to his descendants, and my friend Tanuma was the last in line to receive the heirlooms.

Although episodes concerning Tanuma's craze for mirrors and lenses in his boyhood are almost endless, those I remember most vividly took place in the latter part of his high-school days, when he was deeply involved in the study of physics, especially optics.

One day while we were in the classroom (Tanuma and I were classmates in the same school), the teacher passed around a concave mirror and invited all the students to

7

observe the reflection of their faces in the glass. When my turn came to look I recoiled with horror, for the numerous festering pimples on my face, so greatly magnified, looked exactly like craters on the moon seen through the gigantic telescope of an astronomical observatory. I might mention that I had always been extremely sensitive about my heavily pimpled face, so much so that the shock I received on this occasion left me with a phobia of looking into such concave mirrors. On one occasion not long after this incident I happened to visit a science exhibition, but when I spotted an extra-large concave mirror mounted in the far distance I took to my heels in holy terror.

Tanuma, however, in sharp contrast to my sensitive feelings, let out a shrill cry of joy as soon as he got his first glance at that concave mirror in the classroom. "Wonderful . . . wonderful !" he shrieked, and all the other students laughed at him.

But to Tanuma the experience was no laughing matter, for he was in dead earnest. Subsequently his love for concave mirrors grew so intense that he was for ever buying all sorts of paraphernalia – wire, cardboard, mirrors, and the like. From these he mischievously began constructing various devilish trick-boxes with the help of many books which he had procured, all devoted to the art of scientific magic.

Following Tanuma's graduation from high school, he showed no inclination to pursue his academic studies further. Instead, with the money which was generously supplied him by his easy-going parents, he built a small laboratory in one corner of his garden and devoted his full time and effort to his craze for optical instruments.

He completely isolated himself in his weird laboratory, and I was the only friend who ever visited him, the others having all given him up because of his growing eccentricity. On each visit I began to feel more and more anxious over his strange doings, for I could see clearly that his malady was going from bad to worse.

8

About this time both his parents died, leaving him with a handsome inheritance. Now completely free from any supervision, and with ample funds to satisfy his every whim, he began to grow more reckless than ever. At the same time, having now reached the age of twenty, he began to show a keen interest in the opposite sex. This interest intermingled with his morbid craze for optics, and the two grew into a powerful force in which he was completely enmeshed.

Immediately after receiving his inheritance he built a small observatory and equipped it with an astronomical telescope in order to explore the mysteries of the planets. As his house stood on a high elevation, it was an ideal spot for this purpose. But he was not one to be satisfied with such an innocuous occupation. Soon he began to turn his telescope earthwards and to focus the lens on the houses of the surrounding area. Fences and other barriers constituted no obstacle, because his observatory stood on very high ground.

The occupants of the neighbouring houses, utterly unaware of Tanuma's prying eyes peering through his telescope, went about their daily lives without any reserve, their sliding paper windows wide open, As a result Tanuma derived hitherto unknown pleasures from his secret explorations into the private lives of his neighbours. One evening he kindly invited me to take a look, but what I saw made my blush a deep crimson, and I refused to partake any more in his observations.

Not long after, he built a special type of periscope which enabled him to get a full view of the rooms of his many young maidservants while he was sitting in his lab. Unaware of this, the maids showed no restraint in whatever they did in the privacy of their own rooms.

Another episode, which I can never erase from my mind, concerned insects. Tanuma began studying them under a small microscope, deriving childish delight from watching both their fighting and their mating. One particular scene which I had the misfortune of seeing was that of a crushed flea. This was a gory sight indeed, for, magnified a thousand-fold, it looked like a large wild boar struggling in a pool of blood.

Some time after this, when I called on Tanuma one afternoon and knocked on his laboratory door, there was no answer. So I casually walked in, as was my custom. Inside, it was completely dark, for all the windows were draped with black curtains. And then suddenly on the large wall ahead of me there appeared some blurred and indescribable object, so monstrous in size that it covered the entire space. I was so startled that I stood transfixed.

Gradually the "thing" on the wall began to take definite shape. The first thing that came into focus was a swamp overgrown with black weeds. Beneath it there appeared two immense eyes the size of washtubs, with brown pupils glinting horribly, while at their sides there flowed many rivers of blood on a white plateau. Next came two large caves, from which there seemed to protrude the black bushy ends of large brooms. These, of course, were the hairs growing in the cavities of a gigantic nose. Then followed two thick lips, which looked like two large, crimson cushions; and they kept moving, exposing two rows of white teeth the proportions of roof-tiles.

It was a picture of a human face. Somehow I thought I recognized the features despite their grotesque size.

Just at this point I heard someone calling: "Don't be alarmed! It's only me!" The voice gave me another shock, for the large lips moved in synchronization with the words, and the eyes seemed to smile.

Abruptly, without any warning, the room was filled with light, and the apparition on the wall vanished. Almost simultaneously Tanuma emerged from behind a curtain at the rear of the room.

Grinning mischievously, he came up to me and exclaimed with childish pride: "Wasn't that a remarkable show?" While I continued to stand motionless, still speechless with wonder, he explained to me that what I had seen was an image of his own face, thrown on the wall by means of a stereopticon which he had had specially constructed to project the human face.

Several weeks later he started another new experiment. This time he built a small room within the laboratory, the interior of which was completely lined with mirrors. The four walls, plus floor and ceiling, were mirrors. Hence, anyone who went inside would be confronted with reflections of every portion of his body; and as the six mirrors reflected one another, the reflections multiplied and re-multiplied *ad infinitum*. Just what the purpose of the room was Tanuma never explained. But I do rememLer that he invited me on one occasion to enter it. I flatly refused, for I was terrified. But from what the servants told me Tanuma frequently entered the "chamber of mirrors" together with Kimiko, his favourite maid, a buxom girl of eighteen, to enjoy the hidden delights of mirrorland.

The servants also told me that at other times he would enter the chamber alone, staying for many minutes, often as long as an hour. Once he had stayed inside so long that the servants had become alarmed. One of them mustered up enough courage to knock on the door. Tanuma came leaping out, stark naked, and without even a word of explanation, fled to his own room.

I must explain at this juncture that Tanuma's health was fast deteriorating. On the other hand, his craze for optical instruments kept increasing in intensity. Continuing to spend his fortune on his insane hobby, he kept laying in bigger and bigger stocks of mirrors of all shapes and descriptions – concave, convex, corrugated, prismatic – as well as miscellaneous specimens that cast completely distorted reflections. Finally, however, he reached the stage where he could no longer find any further satisfaction unless he himself manufactured his own mirrors. So he established a glass-working plant in his spacious garden, and there, with the help of a select staff of technicians and workmen, began turning out all kinds of fantastic mirrors. He had no relative to restrain him in his insane ventures, and the handsome wages he paid his servants assured their complete obedience. Hence I felt it was my duty to try and dissuade him from squandering any more of his fast-dwindling fortune. But Tanuma would not listen to me.

I was nevertheless determined to keep an eye on him, fearing he might lose his mind completely, and visited him frequently. And on each occasion I was a witness to some still madder example of his mirror-making orgy, each example becoming more and more difficult to describe.

One of the things he did was to cover one whole wall of his laboratory with a giant mirror. Then in the mirror he cut out five holes; he would thrust his arms, legs, and head through these holes from the back side of the mirror, creating a weird illusion of a trunkless body floating in space.

On other occasions I would find his lab cluttered up with a miscellaneous collection of mirrors of fantastic shapes and sizes – corrugated, concave and convex types predominating – and he would be dancing in their midst, completely naked, in the manner of some primitive pagan ritualist or witch doctor. Every time I beheld these scenes I got the shivers, for the reflection of his madly whirling naked body became contorted and twisted into a thousand variations. Sometimes his head would appear double, his lips swollen to immense proportions; again his belly would swell and rise, then flatten out; his swinging arms would multiply like those found on ancient Chinese Buddhist statues. Indeed, during such times the laboratory was transformed into a purgatory of freaks.

Next, Tanuma rigged up a gigantic kaleidoscope which seemed to fill the entire length of his laboratory. This was rotated by a motor, and with each rotation of the giant cylinder the mammoth flower patterns of the kaleidoscope would change in form and hue – red, pink, purple, green, vermilion, black – like the flowers of an opium addict's dream. And Tanuma himself would crawl into the cylinder, dancing there crazily among the flowers, his stark naked body and limbs multiplying like the petals of the flowers, making it seem as if he, too, were one of the flowery features of the kaleidoscope.

Nor did his madness end here – far from it. His fantastic creations multiplied rapidly, each on a larger scale than the previous one. Until about this time I had still believed that he was partly sane; but finally even I had to admit he had completely lost his mind. And shortly thereafter came the terrible, tragic climax.

One morning I was suddenly awakened by an excited messenger from Tanuma's house.

"A terrible thing has happened! Miss Kimiko wants you to come immediately!" the messenger cried, his face white as a sheet of rice-paper.

"What's the matter?" I asked, hurriedly getting into my clothes.

"We don't know yet," exclaimed the servant. "But for God's sake, come with me at once!"

I tried to question the servant further, but he was so incoherent that I gave up and hurried as fast as I could to Tanuma's laboratory.

Entering the eerie place, the first person I saw was Kimiko, the attractive young parlourmaid whom Tanuma had made his mistress. Near her stood several of the other maids, all huddled together and gazing horror-struck at a large spherical object reposing in the centre of the room.

This sphere was abc̄ut twice as large as the ball on which circus clowns often balance themselves. The exterior was completely covered with white cloth. What terrified me was the fantastic way this sphere kept rolling slowly and haphazardly, as if it were alive. Far more terrible, however, was the strange noise that echoed faintly from the interior of the ball – it was a laugh, a spine-chilling laugh that seemed to come from the throat of a creature from some other world.

"What – what's going on? What in the word is happening?" I asked the stunned group.

"We – we don't know," one of the maids replied dazedly. "We think our master's inside. But we can't do anything. We've called several times, but there's been no answer except the weird laughter you hear now."

Hearing this, I approached the sphere gingerly, trying to find out how the sounds got out of the sphere. Soon I discovered several small air holes. Pressing my eye to one of these small openings, I peered inside; but I was blinded by a brilliant light and could see nothing clearly. However, I *did* ascertain one thing – there was a creature inside!

"Tanuma! Tanuma!" I called out several times, putting my mouth against the hole. But the same weird laughter was all that I could hear.

Not knowing what to do next, I stood, uncertainly watching the ball roll about. And then suddenly I noticed the thin lines of a square partition on the smooth exterior surface. I realized at once that this was a door, allowing entry into the sphere. "But if it's a door, where's the knob?" I asked myself. Examining the door carefully, I saw a small screw-hole which must have held some kind of a handle.

At the sight of this I was struck by a terrible thought. "It's quite possible," I told myself, "that the handle has accidentally come loose, trapping inside whoever it is that entered the sphere. If so, the man must have spent the entire night inside, unable to get out."

Searching the floor of the laboratory, I soon found a T-shaped handle. I tried to fit it to the hole, but it would not work, for the stem was broken.

I could not understand why in the world the man inside – if indeed it was a man – didn't shout and scream for help instead of letting out those weird chuckles and laughs. "Maybe," I suddenly reminded myself with a start, "Tanuma is inside and has gone stark raving mad."

I quickly decided that there was but one thing to do. I

hurried to the glass works, picked up a heavy hammer, and rushed back into the lab. Aiming carefully, I brought the hammer down on the globe with all my might. Again and again I struck at the strange object, and it was soon reduced to a mass of thick fragments of glass.

The man who crawled out of the debris was indeed none other than Tanuma. But he was almost unrecognizable, for he had undergone a horrible transformation. His face was pulpy and discoloured; his eyes kept wandering aimlessly; his hair was a shaggy tangle; his mouth was agape, the saliva dripping down in thin, foamy ribbons. His entire expression was that of a raving maniac.

Even the girl Kimiko recoiled with horror after taking one glance at this monstrosity of a man. Needless to say, Tanuma had gone completely insane.

"But how did this come about?" I asked myself. "Could the mere fact of confinement inside this glass sphere have been enough to drive him mad? Moreover, what was his motive in constructing the globe in the first place?"

Although I questioned the servants still huddled close to me, I could learn nothing, for they all swore they had known nothing of the globe, not even that it had existed.

As though completely oblivious of his whereabouts, Tanuma began to wander about the room, still grinning. Kimiko overcame her initial fright with great effort and tearfully tugged at his sleeves. Just at this moment the chief engineer of the glass works arrived on the scene to report for work.

Ignoring his shock at what he saw, I started to fire questions at him relentlessly. The man was so bewildered that he could barely stammer out his replies. But this is what he told me :

A long time ago Tanuma had ordered him to construct this glass sphere. Its walls were half an inch thick and its diameter about four feet. In order to make the interior a one-unit mirror, Tanuma had the workmen and engineers.

paint the exterior of the globe with quicksilver, over which they pasted several layers of cotton cloth. The interior of the globe had been built in such a way that there were small cavities here and there as receptacles for electric bulbs which would not protrude. Another feature of the globe was a door just large enough to permit the entrance of an average-sized man.

The engineers and workers had been completely unaware of the purpose of the product, but orders were orders, and so they had gone ahead with their assignment. At last, on the night before, the globe had been finished, complete with an extra-long electric cord fitted to a socket on the outer surface, and it had been carefully brought into the lab. They plugged the cord into a wall socket, and then departed at once, leaving Tanuma alone with the sphere. What happened later was, of course, beyond the realm of their knowledge.

After hearing the chief engineer's story, I asked him to leave. Then, putting Tanuma in the custody of the servants, who led him away to the house proper, I continued to stand alone in the laboratory, my eyes fixed on the glass fragments scattered about the room, desperately trying to solve the mystery of what had happened.

For a long while I stood thus, wrestling with the conundrum. Finally I reached the conclusion that Tanuma, after having completely exhausted every new idea in his mania of optics, had decided that he would construct a glass globe, completely lined with a single-unit mirror, which he would enter in order to see his own reflection.

Why would a man become crazy if he entered a glass globe lined with a mirror? What in the name of the devil had he seen there? When these thoughts passed through my mind, I felt as if I had been stabbed through the spine with a sword of ice.

Did he go mad after taking a glance at himself reflected by a completely spherical mirror? Or did he slowly lose his sanity after suddenly discovering that he was trapped inside his horrible round glass coffin – together with "that" reflection?

What, then, I asked myself again, had he seen? It was surely something completely beyond the scope of human imagination. Assuredly, never before had anyone shut himself up within the confines of a mirror-lined sphere. Even a trained physicist could not have guessed exactly what sort of vision would be created inside that sphere. Probably it would be a thing so unthinkable as to be utterly out of this world of ours.

So strange and terrifying must have been this reflection, of whatever shape it was, as it filled Tanuma's complete range of vision, that it would have made any mortal insane.

The only thing we know is the reflection cast by a concave mirror, which is only one section of a spherical whole. It is a monstrously huge magnification. But who could possibly imagine what the result would be when one is wrapped up in a complete succession of concave mirrors?

My hapless friend, undoubtedly, had tried to explore the regions of the unknown, violating sacred taboos, thereby incurring the wrath of the gods. By trying to pry open the secret portals of forbidden knowledge with his weird mania of optics he had destroyed himself.

THE CATERPILLAR
by Edogawa Rampo

TOKIKO said good-bye, left the main house, and went into the twilight through the wide, utterly neglected garden overgrown with weeds, towards the detached cottage where she and her husband lived. While walking, she recalled the conventional words of praise which had again been bestowed upon her a few moments ago by the retired major general who was the master of the main house.

Somehow she felt very queer, and a bitter taste much akin to that of broiled eggplant, which she positively detested, remained in her mouth.

"The loyalty and meritorious services of Lieutenant Sunaga are of course the boast of our Army," he had stated. (The old general was ludicrous enough to continue to dignify her disabled soldier husband with his old title.)

"As for you, however, your continued faithfulness has deprived you of all your former pleasures and desires. For three long years you have sacrificed everything for that poor crippled man, without emitting the faintest breath of complaint. You always contend that this is but the natural duty of a soldier's wife, and so it is. But I sometimes cannot help feeling that it's a cruel fate for a woman to endure, especially for a woman so very attractive and charming as you, and so young, too. I am quite struck with admiration. I honestly believe it to be one of the most stirring human-interest stories of the day. The question which still remains is: How long will it last? Remember, you still have quite a long future ahead of you. For your husband's sake, I pray that you will never change."

Old Major General Washio always liked to sing the praises of the disabled Lieutenant Sunaga (who had once been on his staff and was now his guest tenant) and his wife, so much so that it had become a well-rehearsed line of conversation whenever he saw her. But this was all extremely distasteful to Tokiko, and she tried to avoid the general as much as possible. Occasionally, when the tedium of life with her silent, crippled husband became unbearable, she would seek the company of the general's wife and daughter, but usually only after first making sure that the general was absent.

Secretly, she felt that her self-sacrificing spirit and rare faithfulness well deserved the old man's lavish praise, and at first this had tickled her vanity. But in those early days the whole arrangement had been a novelty. Then it had even been fun, in a way, to care for one so completely helpless as her husband.

Gradually, however, her self-satisfaction had begun to change into boredom, and then into fear. Now she shuddered whenever she was highly praised. She imagined she could see an accusing finger pointing at her, while in her ear she heard a sarcastic voice rasping: "Under the cloak of faithfulness you are leading a life of sin and treachery!"

Day by day the unconscious changes which took place in her way of thinking surprised even herself. In fact, she often wondered at the fickleness of human feelings.

In the beginning she had been only a humble and faithful wife, ignorant of the world, naïve and bashful in the extreme. But now, although her outward appearance showed little change, horrible passions dwelt in her heart, passions awakened by the constant sight of her pitiful, crippled husband – he was so crippled that the word was utterly inappropriate to describe his condition – he who had once been so proud, and of such a noble bearing.

Like a beast of prey, or as if possessed by the devil, she had begun to feel an insane urge to gratify her lust! Yes, she had changed – so completely! From where did this maddening impulse spring, she asked herself. Could it be attributed to the mysterious charm of that lump of flesh? As a matter of fact, that is all her husband was – just a lump of flesh! Or was it the work of some uncanny, supernatural power which could not be defined?

Whenever General Washio spoke to her, Tokiko could not help feeling conscious of this inexplicable sense of guilt. Furthermore, she became more and more conscious of her own large and fat body.

"An alarming situation," she kept repeating. "Why do I continue to grow so fat like some lazy fool?" In sharp contrast, however, her countenance was very pale, and she often seemed to sense that the general looked upon her body dubiously while uttering his usual words of praise. Perhaps this was why she detested him.

It was a remote district where they lived, and the distance from the main house to the cottage was almost half a city block. Between the houses there was a grassy field with no regular paths, where striped snakes often crawled out with rustling noises. Also, if one took a false step, he was immediately in danger of falling into an old abandoned well covered with weeds.

An uneven apology for a hedge surrounded the large mansion, with fields sprawling beyond it.

From the darkness where she stood Tokiko eyed the gaunt, two-storied cottage, their abode, with its back towards the far grove of a small Buddhist shrine. In the sky a couple of stars seemed to twinkle a little more brightly than the others. The room where her husband lay was dark. He was naturally unable to light the lamp, and so the "lump of flesh" must be blinking his eyes helplessly, leaning back in his squat chair, or slipping off the seat to lie on the mats in the gloom.

What a pity! When she thought of it, chills of disgust, misery, and sorrow seemed to run down her spine.

Entering the house, she noticed that the door of the room upstairs was ajar, gaping like a wide black mouth, and she heard the familir low sound of tapping on the mats.

"Oh, he is at it again," she said to herself, and she suddenly felt so sorry for him that tears sprang to her eyes. These sounds meant that her disabled husband was lying on his back, calling impatiently for his only companion by beating his head against the matted floor instead of clapping hands like any ordinary Japanese husband would.

"I'm coming now. You must be hungry." She spoke softly in her usual manner, even though she knew that she could not be heard. Then she climbed the ladder-like stairs to the small room on the second floor.

In the room there was an alcove, with an old-fashioned lamp in one corner. Beside it there was a box of matches, but he was unable to strike a light.

In the tone of a mother speaking to her baby, she said: "I've kept you waiting a long time, haven't I? I'm so sorry." Then she added: "Be patient now for just a moment. I can do nothing in this darkness. I'm going to light the lamp."

Although she kept muttering thus, she knew her husband could hear nothing. After lighting the lamp, she brought it to the desk in another corner of the room. In front of the desk was a low chair, to which was fastened a printed-muslin cushion. The chair was vacant, and its erstwhile occupant was now on the matted floor – a strange, gruesome creature. It was dressed – "was wrapped" might be more appropriate – in old silken robes.

Yes, there "it" was, a large, living parcel wrapped in silken kimono, looking like a parcel which someone had discarded, a queer bundle indeed!

From one part of the parcel protruded the head of a man, which kept tapping against the mat like a spring-beetle or

20

some strange automatic machine. As it tapped, the large bundle moved bit by bit . . . like a crawling worm.

"You mustn't lose your temper like that. What do you want? This?" She made the gesture of taking food. "No? Then this?" She tried another gesture, but her mute husband shook his head every time and continued to knock his head desperately against the matting.

His whole face had been so badly shattered by the splinters of a shell that it was just like a mass of putty. Only upon close observation could one recognize it as once having been a human face.

The left ear was entirely gone, and only a small black hole showed where it had once been. From the left side of his mouth across his cheek to beneath his eyes there was a pronounced twitch like a suture, while an ugly scar also crept across his right temple up to the top of his head. His throat caved in as if the flesh there had been scooped out, while his nose and mouth retained nothing of their original shapes.

In this monstrous face, however, there were still set two bright, round eyes like those of an innocent child, contrasting sharply with the ugliness around them. Just now they were gleaming with irritation.

"Ah! You want to say something to me, don't you? Wait a minute."

She took a notebook and pencil out of the drawer of the desk, put the pencil in his deformed mouth and held the opened notebook against it. Her husband could neither speak nor hold a pen, for as he had no vocal organs, he likewise had no arms or legs.

"Tired of me?" These were the words the cripple scrawled with his mouth.

"Ho, ho, ho! You're jealous again, aren't you?" she laughed. "Don't be a little fool."

But the cripple again began to strike his head impatiently against the mat floor. Tokiko understood what he meant and again pressed the notebook against the point of the pencil held between his teeth.

Once more the pencil moved unsteadily and wrote: "Where go?"

As soon as she looked at it, Tokiko roughly snatched the pencil away from the man's mouth, wrote: "To the Washios'," and almost pushed the written reply against his eyes.

As he read the curt note, she added: "You should know! What other place have I to go?"

1

The cripple again called for the notebook and wrote: "3 hours?"

A surge of sympathy again swept over her. "I didn't realize I was away so long," she wrote back. "I'm sorry."

She expressed her pity, bowed, and waved her hand, saying: "I won't go again. I won't ever go again. I promise."

Lieutenant Sunaga, or rather "the bundle," still seemed far from satisfied, but perhaps he became tired of the performance of writing with his mouth, for his head lay limp on the floor and moved no more. After a brief spell, he looked hard at her, putting every meaning into his large eyes.

Tokiko knew just one way to soothe her husband's temper. As words and excuses were of no avail, whenever they had their strange "lovers' quarrels," she resorted to this more expedient act.

Suddenly bending over her husband, she smothered his twisted mouth with kisses. Soon, a look of deep contentment and pleasure crept into his eyes, followed by an ugly smile. She continued to kiss him – closing her eyes in order to forget his ugliness – and, gradually, she felt a strong urge to tease this poor cripple, who was so utterly helpless.

The cripple, kissed with such passion, writhed in the agony of being unable to breathe and distorted his face oddly. As always, this sight excited Tokiko strangely

In the medical world the case of Lieutenant Sunaga had created quite a stir. His arms and legs had been amputated and his face skilfully patched up by the surgeons. As for the newspapers, they had also played up the story, and one journal had even spoken of him as "the pathetic broken doll whose precious limbs were cruelly torn off by the playful gods of war."

Lieutenant Sunaga was all the more pitiful in that, although he was a fourfold amputee, his torso was extremely well developed. Possibly because of his keen appetite – eating was his only diversion – Sunaga's belly was glossy and bulging. In fact, the man was just like a large yellow caterpillar.

His arms and legs had been amputated so closely that not even stumps remained, but only four lumps of flesh to mark where his limbs had been. Often he would lie on his great belly and, using these lumps to propel himself, manage to spin round and round – a top made of living flesh.

After a time Tokiko began to strip him naked. He offered no resistance, but just lay looking expectantly into those strangely narrowed eyes of hers, like the eyes with which an animal watches its prey.

Tokiko well understood what her crippled husband wanted to say with his amorous eyes. Lieutenant Sunaga had lost every sensory organ except those of sight, feeling, and taste. He had never had much liking for books, and furthermore, his wits had been dulled by the shock of the explosion to which he had fallen victim. So now even the pastime of reading had been given up, and physical pleasures were his only diversion.

As for Tokiko, although hers was a timid heart, she had always entertained a strange liking for bullying the weak. Moreover, watching the agony of this poor cripple aroused many of her hidden impulses.

Still leaning over him, she continued her aberrant caresses, stirring the crippled man's feelings to ever higher frenzies of passion. . . .

Tokiko shrieked and woke up. She had had a terrible nightmare, and now she found herself sitting up in a cold sweat. The lamp at her bedside was blackened with smoke, the wick burned down to its base.

The interior of the room, the ceilings, the walls . . . all seemed to be stretching like rubber, and then contracting into strange shapes. The face of her husband beside her was of a glossy orange hue.

She reminded herself that he positively could not have heard her shriek, but she noticed with uneasiness that he was gazing at the ceiling, his bright eyes wide open. She looked at the clock on the desk and noted that it was a little past one.

Now that she was wide awake she tried to erase all thoughts of the horrors of the nightmare that had assailed her mind, but the more she tried to forget, the more persistent became the images. First a mist seemed to rise before her eyes, and when this cleared, she could distinctly see a large lump of flesh, floating in mid-air, spinning and spinning like a top. Suddenly a stout, ugly woman's body seemed to appear from nowhere, and the two figures became interlocked in a mad embrace. The weirdly erotic scene reminded Tokiko of a picture postcard portraying a section of Dante's Inferno; and yet, as her mind drifted, the very disgust and ugliness of the embracing pair seemed to excite all her pent-up passions and to paralyse her nerves. With a shudder she asked herself if she were sexually perverted.

Holding her breasts, she suddenly uttered a piercing cry. Then she looked at her husband intently, like a child gazing at a broken doll. He was still looking at the same spot on the ceiling, taking absolutely no notice of her.

"He is thinking again," she told herself.

Even at the best of times it was an eerie thing to see a man whose only organ of communication was his eyes lie there with those eyes fixed forever on just one spot, and now how much more so in the middle of the night. Of course his mind has become dull, she thought, but for a man so completely crippled as he, there undoubtedly exists a world completely different from any I can ever know. Is it a pleasant world, she wondered. Or is it a hell....

For a while she closed her eyes again and tried to sleep, but she found it impossible. She felt as if flames were whirling around her with roaring sounds, and her mind ached. Time and again various illusions and hallucinations would wantonly appear and then vanish. Into them were woven the manifold tragic happenings which had changed her normal life into this miserable existence since three years back....

When she first received the news that her husband had been wounded and would be sent back to Japan, she felt indescribably relieved to know that at least his life had been spared. The wives of his fellow officers even envied her "good fortune."

Presently the distinguished services rendered by her husband were written up in the newspapers. She knew at the time that his wounds were serious, but she never imagined for a moment that he had been crippled to such an extent.

Never would she forget the first time she was permitted to visit her husband in the garrison hospital. His face was completely covered with bandages, and there was nothing but his eyes, gazing at her vacantly. She remembered how bitterly she wept when they told her that his wounds and the shock had left him both deaf and dumb. Little did she dream, however, of the horrible discoveries that were still to come.

The head physician, dignified as he was, tried to appear deeply sympathetic and turned up the white bed-sheets cautiously. "Try to be brave!" were his very words.

She tried to clasp her husband's hands – but could find no arms. Then she discovered that his legs were also missing; he was like a ghost in a bad dream. Beneath the sheets there lay only his trunk, bandaged grotesquely, like a mummy.

She tried to speak, and then to scream, but no sounds came out of her throat. She, too, had been rendered momentarily speechless. God! Was this all that was left of the husband she loved so dearly! He was no longer a man, but only a plaster bust.

It was after she had been shown to another room by the head physician and nurses that she completely broke down, bursting into loud weeping despite the presence of the others. Throwing herself down on a chair, she buried her head in her arms and wept till her tear-cups ran utterly dry.

"It was a real miracle," she heard the physician say. "No other person could possibly have survived. Of course it's all the result of Colonel Kitamura's wonderful surgical skill – he's a real genius with the operating knife. There's probably no other such example in any garrison hospital in any country."

Thus the physician tried to console Tokiko. The word "miracle" was continually repeated, but she did not know whether to rejoice or grieve.

About half a year had passed in a dream. The "living corpse" of Lieutenant Sunaga was eventually escorted home by his commanding officer and comrades in arms, and everyone made quite a fuss over him.

In the days that followed, Tokiko nursed him with tender care, shedding endless tears. Relatives, neighbours, and friends all urged her on to greater self-sacrifice, constantly dinning their definitions of "honour" and "virtue" into her ears. Her husband's meagre pension was scarcely enough to keep them, so when Major General Washio, Sunaga's former commanding officer at the front, kindly offered to let them live in the detached cottage on his country estate free of charge, they accepted gratefully.

From then on their daily life became routine, but this too brought maddening loneliness. The quiet environment, of course, was a prime cause. Another was the fact that people were no longer interested in the story of the crippled war hero and his dutiful wife. It was stale news; new personalities and events were commanding their interest.

Her husband's relatives seldom came to call. On her side, both her parents were dead, while all her sisters and brothers were indifferent to her sorrows. As a result the poor crippled soldier and his faithful wife lived alone in the solitary cottage in the country, completely isolated from the outside world. But even this state of affairs would not have been so bad if one of them had not been like a doll made of clay.

Lieutenant Sunaga was at first quite confused. Although aware of his tragic plight, his gradual return to normal health brought with it feelings of remorse, melancholy, and complete despair.

Whatever Tokiko and her husband said to each other was through the medium of the written word. The first words he wrote were "newspaper" and "decoration." By the first he meant that he wanted to see the clippings of the papers which had carried the story of his glorious record; and by "decoration" he was asking to see the Order of the Golden Kite, Japan's highest military decoration, which he had been awarded. These had been the first things Major General Washio had thrust before his eyes when he had recovered consciousness at the hospital, and he remembered them.

After that the crippled man often wrote the same words and asked for the two items, and each time Tokiko held them before him, while he gazed long at them. Tokiko felt rather silly while he read the newspapers over and over, but she did derive some pleasure from the look of deep satisfaction in her husband's eyes. Often she held the clippings and the decoration until her hands became quite numb.

As time passed, Lieutenant Sunaga became bored with the term "honour". After a while he no longer asked for the relics of his war record. Instead, his requests turned more and more frequently towards food, for despite his deformity, his appetite grew ever larger. In fact, he was as greedy for food as a patient recovering from some alimentary disorder. If Tokiko did not immediately comply with his request, he would give vent to his temper by crawling about madly on the mats.

At first Tokiko felt a vague fear of his uncouth manners and disliked them, but in time she grew used to his strange whims. With the two completely shut up in the solitary cottage in the country, if one of them had not compromised, life would have become unbearable. So, like two animals caged in a zoo, they pursued their lonely existence.

Thus, from every viewpoint, it was only natural that Tokiko should come to look upon her husband as a big toy, to be played with as she pleased. Furthermore, her crippled husband's greed had infected her own character to the point where she too had become extremely avaricious.

There seemed to be but one consolation for her miserable "career" as nursemaid to a cripple: the very fact that this poor, strange thing which not only could neither speak nor hear, but could not even move freely by itself, was by no means made of wood or clay, but was alive and real, possessing every human emotion and instinct – this was a source of boundless fascination for her. Still further, those round eyes of his, which comprised his only expressive organ, speaking so sadly sometimes, and sometimes so angrily – these too had a strange charm. The pitiful thing was that he was incapable of wiping away the tears which those eyes could still shed. And of course, when he was angry, he had no power to threaten her other than that of working himself into an abnormal heat of frenzy. These fits of wrath usually came on whenever he was reminded that he would never again be able to succumb, of his own free will, to the one overwhelming temptation which was always lurking within him.

Meanwhile Tokiko also managed to find a secondary source of pleasure in tormenting this helpless creature whenever she felt like it. Cruel? Yes! But it was fun – great fun!...

These happenings of the past three years were vividly reflected inside Tokiko's closed eyelids, as though cast by a magic lantern, the fragmentary memories forming themselves in her mind and fading away one after the other. This was a phenomenon which occurred whenever there was something wrong with her body. On such occasions, especially during her monthly periods of physical indisposition, she would maltreat the poor cripple with real venom. The barbarity of her actions had grown wilder and more intense with the progress of time. She was, of course, fully aware of the criminal nature of her deeds, but the wild forces rising inside her body were beyond the control of her will.

Suddenly she felt that the interior of the room was becoming darker, that another nightmare was about to overtake her. But this time she determined to see it with her eyes open. The thought frightened her, and her heart began to skip beats. But she calmed her mind and persuaded herself that she was prone to imagine things. The wick of the lamp at her bedside was spent, and the light was flickering. Climbing out of bed, she turned the wick high.

Quickly the room brightened up, but the light of the lamp was blurred in colours of orange, and this increased her uneasiness. By the same light Tokiko looked again at her husband's face, and was startled to see that his eyes were still fixed on the same spot on the ceiling, not having changed position even a fraction of an inch!

"What could he possibly be thinking about?" she asked herself with a shiver. Although she felt extremely uneasy, hers was even more a feeling of intense hatred of his attitude. Her hatred again awakened all her inherent desires to torment him – to make him suffer.

Suddenly, without any warning, she threw herself upon her husband's bed, grabbed his shoulders with her large hands, and began to shake him furiously.

Startled by this sudden violence, the crippled man began to tremble. Biting his lip, he stared at her fiercely.

27

"Are you angry? Why do you look at me like that?" Tokiko asked sarcastically. "It's no use getting angry, you know! You're quite at my mercy."

Sunaga could not reply, but the words that might have come to his lips showed from his penetrating eyes.

"Your eyes are mad!" Tokiko shrieked. "Don't stare at me like that!"

On a sudden impulse she thrust her fingers roughly into his eyes, shouting: "Now try to stare if you can!"

The cripple struggled desperately, his torso writhing and twisting, and his intense suffering finally gave him the strength to lift his trunk and send her sprawling backwards.

Quickly Tokiko regained her balance and turned to resume her attack. But suddenly she stopped. . . . Horror of horrors! From both her husband's eyes blood was spurting; his face, twitching in pain, had the pallor of a boiled octopus.

Tokiko was paralysed with fear. She had cruelly deprived her husband of his only window to the outside world. What was left to him now? Nothing, absolutely nothing . . . just this mass of ghastly flesh, in total darkness.

Stumbling downstairs, she staggered out into the dark night barefooted. Passing through the back gate of the garden, she rushed out onto the village road, running as though in a nightmare pursued by spectres – fast and yet seeming not to move.

Eventually she reached her destination – the lone house of a country doctor. After hearing her hysterical story, the doctor accompanied her back to the cottage.

In the room her husband was still struggling violently, suffering the tortures of hell. The doctor had often heard of the limbless man, but had never seen him before; he was shocked beyond words by the gruesome sight of the cripple. After giving him an injection to relieve his pain, he dressed the blinded eyes and then hurried away, not even asking for any explanation of the "accident."

By the time Lieutenant Sunaga stopped struggling it was already dawn. Caressing his chest tenderly, Tokiko shed big drops of tears and implored: "Forgive me, my darling. Please forgive me."

The lump of flesh was stricken with fever, its red face swollen and its heart beating rapidly.

Tokiko did not leave the bedside of her patient all day, not even to take any food. She kept squeezing out wet cloths for his head; and in the brief intervals she wrote "Forgive me" again and again on her husband's chest with her finger. She was utterly unconscious of the passing of time.

By evening the patient's temperature showed a slight drop, and his breathing seemed to return to normal. Tokiko surmised he must also have regained consciousness, so again she wrote "Forgive me" on his chest. The lump of flesh, however, made no attempt to make any kind of a reply. Although he had lost his eyes, it would still have been possible for him to answer her signals in some way, either by shaking his head or by smiling. But his facial expression remained unchanged. By the sound of his breathing she knew for sure he was not asleep, but it was impossible to tell whether he had also lost the ability to understand the message traced on his chest or was only keeping silent out of anger.

While gazing at him, Tokiko could not help trembling with terror. This "thing" that lay before her was indeed a living creature. He had lungs and a stomach as well as a heart. Nevertheless, he could not see anything; he could not hear anything; he could not speak a word; he had no limbs. His world was a bottomless pit of perpetual silence and boundless darkness. Who could imagine such a terrible world? With what could the feelings of a man living in that abyss be compared? Surely he must crave to shout for help at the top of his lungs . . . to see shapes, no matter how dim . . . to hear voices, even the faintest of whispers . . . to cling to something . . . to grasp. . . .

Suddenly Tokiko burst out crying with remorse over the irreparable crime she had committed. Fear and sorrow gnawing at her heart, she left her husband there and ran to the Washios in the main house; she wanted to see a human face – any face that was not deformed.

The old general listened anxiously to her long confession, made incoherent at times by fits of weeping, and when she was through he was momentarily too astounded to utter a word. After a while he said he would visit the lieutenant immediately.

As it was already dark, a lantern was prepared for the old man. He and Tokiko plodded through the grassy field towards the cottage, both silent and engrossed in their own thoughts.

When they finally reached the ill-omened room the old man looked inside and then exclaimed: "Nobody's here! Where's he gone?"

Tokiko, however, was not alarmed. "He must be in his bed," she said.

She went to the bed in the semi-gloom, but found it empty.

"No!" she cried. "He – he isn't here!"

"He couldn't have gone out," reasoned the general. "We must search the house."

29

After a thorough search of every nook and corner had proved quite fruitless, General Washio had to admit that his former subordinate was indeed not in the house.

Suddenly Tokiko discovered a pencilled scrawl on one of the paper doors.

"Look!" she said with a puzzled frown, pointing to the scrawl. "What's this?"

They both stooped to look. After a few moments spent deciphering the almost illegible scribble, she made out the message.

"I forgive you!" it said.

Tears immediately welled in Tokiko's eyes, and she began to feel dizzy. It was evident that her husband had managed to drag his truncated body across the room, picked up a pencil from the low desk in his mouth, laboriously written the curt message, and then –

Suddenly Tokoko came alive with action.

"Quick!" she shouted, her face paling. "He may be committing suicide!"

The Washio household was quickly aroused, and soon servants came out with lanterns to search the field. Hither and thither they looked, trampling down the weeds between the main house and the cottage.

Tokiko anxiously followed old man Washio in the dim light of the lantern which he held. While she walked the words "I forgive you" kept leaping to her mind; clearly this was his answer to the message she had traced on his chest. Turning the words over and over in her mind, she came to realize that his message also meant: "I'm going to die. But do not grieve, because I have forgiven you!"

What a heartless witch she had been! In her mind's eye she could vividly see her limbless husband falling down the stairs and crawling out into the darkness. She felt that she would choke with sorrow and remorse.

After they had walked about for some time, a horrible thought struck her. Turning to the general, she ventured: "There is an old well hereabouts, isn't there?"

"Yes," he replied gravely, immediately understanding what she meant.

Both of them hurried in a new direction.

"The well should be around here, I think," said the old man finally, as if talking to himself. Then he held up his lantern to to spread as much light as possible.

Just then Tokiko was struck by some uncanny intuition. She stopped in her tracks. Straining her ears, she heard a faint rustling sound like that made by a snake crawling through the grass.

She and the old man looked towards the sound, and almost simultaneously they both became transfixed with fear.

In the dim light a black thing was wriggling sluggishly in the thick growth of weeds. Suddenly the thing raised its head and crawled forward, scraping the ground with projections like excrescences at the four corners of its body. It advanced stealthily inch by inch.

After a time the upraised head suddenly disappeared into the ground, dragging its whole body after it. A few seconds later they heard the faint sound of a splash far beneath the ground in what seemed like the bowels of the earth.

Tokiko and the general finally mustered enough courage to step forward . . . and there, hidden in the grass, they found the old well, its black mouth gaping.

Strangely enough, in those timeless moments it had been the image of a caterpillar which had flashed again into Tokiko's mind – a bloated creature slowly creeping along the dead branch of a gaunt tree on a dark night . . . inching its way to the end of the branch and then suddenly dropping off . . . falling down . . . down into the boundless darkness beneath.

The Red Stockade

A Story Told by the Old Coastguard

We was on the southern part of the China station, when the 'George Ranger' was ordered to the Straits of Malacca, to put down the pirates that had been showing themselves of late. It was in the forties, when ships was ships, not iron kettles full of wheels, and other devilments, and there was a chance of hand-to-hand fighting – not being blown up in an iron cellar by you don't know who. Ships was ships in them days!

There had been a lot of throat-cutting and scuttling, for them devils stopped at nothing. Some of us had been through the straits before, when we was in the 'Polly Phemus', seventy-four, going to the China station, and although we had never come to quarters with the Malays, we had seen some of their work, and knew what kind they was. So, when we had left Singapore in the 'George Ranger' – for that was our saucy, little thirty-eight-gun frigate – the place wasn't in them days what it is now – many and many's the yarn was told in the fo'c'sle, and on the watches, of what the yellow devils could do, and had done. Some of us took it one way, and some another, but all, save a few, wanted to get into hand-grips with the pirates, for all their kreeses, and their stinkpots, and the devil's engines what they used. There was some that didn't mind cold steel of an ordinary kind, and would have faced cutlasses and boarding-pikes, any day, for a holiday, but that didn't like the idea of those knives like crooked flames, and that sliced a man in two, and hacked through the bowels of him. Naturally, we didn't take much stock of this kind; and many's the joke we had on them, and some of them cruel enough jokes, too.

You may be sure there was good stories, with plenty of cutting, and blood, and tortures in them, told in their watches, and nigh the whole ship's crew was busy, day and night, remembering and inventing things that'd make them gasp and grow white. I think that, somehow, the captain and the officers must have known what was goin' on, for there came tales from the wardroom that was worse nor any of ours. The midshipmen used to delight in them, like the ship's boys did, and one of them, that had a kreese, used to bring it out when he could, and show how the pirates used it when they cut the hearts out of men and women, and ripped them up to the chins. It was a bit cruel, at times, on them poor, white-livered chaps – a man can't help his liver, I suppose – but, anyhow, there's no place for them in a warship, for they're apt to do more harm by living where there's men of all sorts, than they can do by dying. So there wasn't any mercy for them, and the captain was worse on them than any. Captain Wynyard was him that commanded the corvette 'Sentinel' on the China station, and was promoted to the 'George Ranger' for cutting up a fleet of junks that was hammering at the 'Rajah', from Canton, racing for Southampton with the first of the season's tea. He was a man, if you like, a bulldog full of hellfire, when he was on for fighting; he wouldn't have a white liver at any price. 'God hates a coward,' he said once, 'and under Her Britannic Majesty I'm here to carry out God's will. Trice him up, and give him a dozen!' At least, that's the story they tell of him when he was round Shanghai, and one of his men had held back when the time came for boarding a fire-junk that was coming down the tide. And with that he went in, and steered her off with his own hands.

Well, the captain knew what work there was before us, and that it weren't no time for kid gloves and hair oil, much less a bokey in your buttonhole and a top hat, and he didn't mean that there should be any funk on his ship. So you take your davy that it wasn't his fault if things was made too pleasant aboard for men what feared fallin' into the clutches of the Malays.

Now and then he went out of his way to be nasty over such folk, and, boy or man, he never checked his tongue on a hard word when any one's face was pale before him. There was one old chap on board that we called 'Old Land's End', for he came from that part, and that had a boy of his on the 'Billy Ruffian', when he sailed on her, and after got lost, one night, in cutting out a Greek sloop at Navarino, in 1827. We used to chaff him when there was trouble with any of the boys, for he used to say that his boy might have been in that trouble, too. And now, when the chaff was on about bein' afeered of the Malays, we used to rub it into the old man; but he would flame up, and answer us that his boy died in his duty, and that he couldn't be afeered of nought.

One night there was a row on among the midshipmen, for they said that one of them, Tempest by name, owned up to being afraid of being kreesed. He was a rare bright little chap of about thirteen, that was always in fun and trouble of some kind; but he was soft-hearted, and sometimes the other lads would tease him. He would own up truthfully to anything he thought, or felt, and now they had drawn him to own something that none of them would – no matter how true it might be. Well, they had a rare fight, for the boy was never backward with his fists, and by accident it came to the notice of the captain. He insisted on being told what it was all about, and when young Tempest spoke out, and told him, he stamped on the deck, and called out: 'I'll have no cowards in this ship,' and was going on, when the boy cut in: 'I'm no coward, sir; I'm a gentleman!'

'Did you say you were afraid? Answer me – yes, or no?'

'Yes, sir, I did, and it was true! I said I feared the Malay kreeses; but I did not mean to shirk them, for all that. Henry of Navarre was afraid, but, all the same, he –'

'Henry of Navarre be damned,' shouted the captain, 'and you, too! You said you were afraid, and that, let me tell you, is what we call a coward in the Queen's navy. And if you are one, you can, at least, have the grace to keep it to yourself! No answer to me! To the masthead for the remainder of the day! I want my crew to know what to avoid, and to know it when they see it!' and he walked away, while the lad, without a word, ran up the maintop.

Some way, the men didn't say much about this. The only one that said anything to the point was Old Land's End, and says he: 'That may be a coward, but I'd chance it that he was a boy of mine.'

As we went up the straits and got the sun on us, and the damp heat of that kettle of a place – Lor' bless ye! Ye steam there, all day and all night like a copper at the galley – we began to look around for the pirates, and there wasn't a man that got drowsy on the watch. We coasted along as we went up north, and took a look into the creeks and rivers as we went. It was up these that the Malays hid themselves; for the fevers and such that swept off their betters like flies, didn't seem to have any effect on them. There was pretty bad bits, I tell you, up some of them rivers through the mango groves, where the marshes spread away, mile after mile, as far as you could see, and where everything that is noxious, both beast, and bird, and fish, and crawling thing, and insect, and tree, and bush, and flower, and creeper, is most at home.

But the pirate ships kept ahead of us; or, if they came south again, passed us by in the night, and so we ran up till about the middle of the peninsula, where the worst of the piracies had happened. There we got up as well as we could to look like a ship in distress; and, sure enough, we deceived the beggars, for two of them came out one early dawn and began to attack us. They was ugly looking craft, too – long, low hull and lateen sails, and a double crew twice told in every one of them.

But if the crafts was ugly the men was worse, for uglier devils I never saw. Swarthy, yellow chaps, some of them, and some with shaven crowns and white eyeballs, and others as black as your shoe, with one or two white men, more shame, among them, but all carrying kreeses as long as your arm, and pistols in their belts.

They didn't get much change from us, I tell you. We let them get close, and then gave them a broadside that swept their decks like a hailstorm; but we was unlucky that we didn't grapple them, for they managed to shift off and ran for it. Our boats was out quick, but we daren't follow them where they ran into a wide creek, with mango swamps on each side as far as the eye could reach. The boat came back after a bit and reported that they had run up the river which was deep enough but with a winding channel between great mudbanks, where alligators lay in hundreds. There seemed some sort of fort where the river narrowed, and the pirates ran in behind it and disappeared up the bend of the river.

Then the preparations began. We knew that we had got two craft, at any rate, caged in the river, and there was every chance that we had found their lair. Our captain wasn't one that let things go asleep, and by daylight the next morning we was ready for an attack. The pinnace and four other boats started out under the first lieutenant to prospect, and the rest that was left on board waited, as well as they could, till we came back.

That was an awful day. I was in the second boat, and we all kept well together when we began to get into the narrows of the mouth of the river. When we started, we went in a couple of hours after the flood tide, and so all we saw when the light came seemed fresh and watery. But as the tide ran out, and the big black mudbanks began to show their heads above everywhere, it wasn't nice, I can tell you. It was hardly possible for us to tell the channels, for everywhere the tide raced quick, and it was only when the boat began to touch the black slime that you knew that you was on a bank. Twice our boat was almost caught this way, but by good luck we pulled and pushed off in time into the ebbing tide; and hardly a boat but touched somewhere. One that was a bit out from the rest of us got stuck at last in a nasty cut between two mudbanks, and as the water ran away the boat turned over on the slope, despite all her crew could do, and we saw the poor fellows thrown out into the slime. More than one of them began to swim toward us, but behind each came a rush of something dark, and though we shouted and made what noise we could, and fired many shots, the alligators was too close, and with shriek after shriek they went down to the bottom of the filth and slime. Oh, man! it was a dreadful sight, and none the better that it was new to nigh all of us. How it would have taken us if we had time to think about it, I hardly know, but I doubt that more than a few would have grown cold over it; but just then there flew amongst us a hail of small shot from a fleet of boats that had stolen down on us. They drove out from behind a big mudbank that rose steeper than the others and that seemed solider, too, for the gravel of it showed, as the scour of the tide washed the mud away. We was not sorry, I tell you, to have men to fight with, instead of alligators and mudbanks, in an ebbing tide, in a strange tropical river.

We gave chase at once, and the pinnace fired the twelve-pounder which she carried in the bows, in among the huddle of the boats, and the yells arose as the rush of the alligators turned to where the Malay heads bobbed up and down in the drift of the tide. Then the pirates turned and ran, and we after them as hard as we could pull, till round a sharp bend of the river we came to a narrow place, where one side was steep for a bit and then tailed away to a wilderness of marsh, worse than we had seen. The other side was crowned by a sort of fort, built on the top of a high bank, but guarded by a stockade and a mudbank which lay at its base. From this there came a rain of bullets, and we saw some guns turned toward us. We was hardly strong enough to attack such a position without reconnoitring, and so we drew away; but not quite quick enough, for before we could get out of range of their guns a round shot carried away the whole of the starboard oars of one of our boats.

It was a dreary pull to the ship, and the tide was agin us, for we all got thinking of what we had to tell – one boat and crew lost entirely, and a set of oars shot away – and no work done.

The captain was furious; and, in the wardroom, and in the fo'c'sle that night, there was nothing that wasn't flavoured with anger and curses. Even the boys, of all sorts, from the cabin-boys to the midshipmen, was wanting to get at the Malays. However, sharp was the order; and by daylight three boats was up at the stockaded fort, making an accurate survey. I was again in one of the boats; and, in spite of what the captain had said to make us all so angry – and he had a tongue like vitriol, I tell you – we all felt pretty down and cold when we got again amongst those terrible mudbanks and saw the slime that shone on them bubble up, when the grey of the morning let us see anything.

We found that the fort was one that we would have to take if we wanted to follow the pirates up the river, for it barred the way without a chance. There was a gut of the river between the two great ridges of gravel, and this was the only channel where there was a chance of passing. But it had been staked on both sides, so that only the centre was left free. Why, from the fort they could have stoned any one in the boats passing there, only that there wasn't any stone, that we could see, in their whole blasted country!

When we got back, with two cases of sunstroke among us, and reported, the captain ordered preparations for an attack on the fort, and the next morning the ball began. It was ugly work. We got close up to the fort, but, as the tide ran out, we had to sheer away somewhat so as not to get stranded. The whole place swarmed with those grinning devils. They evidently had some way of getting to and from their boats behind the stockade. They did not fire a shot at us – not at first – and that was the most aggravating thing that you can imagine. They seemed to know something that we did not, and they only just waited. As the tide sank lower and lower, and the mudbanks grew steeper, and the sun on them began to fizzle, a steam arose that nigh turned our stomachs. Why, the sight of them alone would make your heart sink!

The slime shimmered in all kinds of colours, like the water when there's tarring work on hand, and the whole place seemed alive with all that was horrible. The alligators kept off the boats and the banks close to us, but the thick water was full of eels and watersnakes, and the mud was alive with water-worms and leeches, and horrible, gaudy-coloured crabs. The very air was filled with pests – flies of all kinds, and a sort of big-striped insect that they call the 'tiger mosquito', which comes out in the daytime and bites you like red-hot pincers. It was bad enough, I tell you, for us men with hair on our faces, but some of the boys got very white and pale, and they was all pretty silent for a while. All at once the crowd of Malays behind the stockade began to roll their eyes and wave their kreeses and to shout. We knew that there was some cause for it, but couldn't make it out, and this exasperated us more than ever. Then the captain sings out to us to attack the stockade; so out we all jumped into the mud. We knew it couldn't be very deep just there, on account of the gravel beneath. We was knee-deep in a moment, but we struggled, and slipped, and fell over each other; and, when we got to the top of that bank, we was the queerest, filthiest-looking crowd you ever see. But the mud hadn't took the heart out of us, and the Malays, with their necks craned over the stockade, and with the nearest thing to a laugh or a smile that the devil lets them have, drew back and fell, one on another, when they heard our cheer.

Between them and us there was a bit of a dip where the water had been running in the ebb tide, but which seemed now as dry as the rest, and the foremost of our men charged down the slope, and then we knew why they had kept silent and waited! We was in a regular trap. The first ranks disappeared at once in the mud and ooze in the hollow, and those next were up to their armpits before they could stop. Then those Malay devils opened on us, and while we tried to pull our chaps out, they mowed us down with every kind of small arm they had – and they had a queer assortment, I tell you.

It was all we could do to get back over the slope and to the boats again – what was left of us – and, as we hadn't hands enough left even to row with full strength, we had to make for the ship as fast as we could, for their boats began to pass out in a cloud through the narrow by the stockade. But before we went we saw them dragging the live and dead out of the mud with hooks on the end of long bamboos; and there was terrible shrieks from some poor fellows when the kreeses gashed through them. We daren't wait; but we saw enough to make us swear revenge. When we saw them devils stick the bleeding heads of our comrades on the spikes of the stockade, there was nigh a mutiny because the captain wouldn't let us go back and have another try for it. He was cool enough now; and those of us that knew him and understood what was in his mind, when the smile on him showed the white teeth in the corners of his mouth, felt that it was no good day's work that the pirates had done for themselves.

When we got back to the ship and told our tale, it wasn't long till the men was all on fire; and nigh every man took a turn with the grindstone at his cutlass, till they was all like razors. The captain mustered every one on board, and detailed every man to his work in the boats, ready for the next time; and we knew that, by daylight, we were to have another slap at the pirates. We got six-pounders and twelve-pounders in most of the boats, for we was to give them a dose of big shot before we came to close quarters.

When we got up near the stockade, the tide had turned, and we thought it better to wait till dawn, for it was bad work among the mudbanks at the ebb in the dark. So we hung on a while, and then when the sky began to lighten, we made for the fort. When we got nigh enough to see it, there wasn't a man of us who didn't want to have some bloody revenge, for there, on the spikes of the stockade, were the heads of all the poor fellows that we had lost the day before, with a cloud of mosquitoes and flies already beginning to buzz around them in the dawn. But beyond that again, they had painted the outside of the stockade with blood, so that the whole place was a crimson mass. You could smell it as the sun came up!

Well, that day was a hard one. We opened fire with our guns, and the Malays returned it, with all they had got. A fleet of boats came out from beyond the fort, and for a while we had to turn our attention to these. The small guns served us well, and we made a rare havoc among the boats, for our shot went crashing through them, and quite a half of them were sunk. The water was full of bobbing heads; but the tide carried them away from us, and their cries and shrieks came from beyond the fort and then died away. The other boats recognized their danger, and turned and ran in through the narrow, and let us alone for hours after. Then we went at the fort again. We turned our guns at the piles of the stockade, and, of course, every shot told – but their fire was at too close quarters, and with their rifles and matchlocks, and the rest, they picked us off too fast, and we had to sheer off where our heavy metal could tell without our being within their range. Before we sheered off, we could see that the hole we had knocked in the stockade was only in the outer work, and that the real fort was within. We had to go down the river, as we couldn't go far enough across without danger from the banks, and this only gave us a side view, and, do what we would, we couldn't make an impression – at least any that we could see.

That was a long and awful day! The sun was blazing on us like a furnace, and we was nigh mad with heat, and flies, and drouth, and anger. It was that hot that if you touched metal it fairly burned you. When the tide was near the flood, the captain ordered up the boats in the wide water now opposite the fort; and there, for a while, we got a fair chance, till, when the ebb began, we should have to sheer off again. By this time our shot was nearly run out, and we thought that we should have to give over; but all at once came order to prepare for attack, and in a few minutes we was working for dear life across the river, straight for the stockade. The men set up a cheer, and the pirates showed over the top of the stockade and waved their kreeses, and more than one of them sliced off pieces of the heads on the spikes, and jeered at us, as much as to say that they would do the same for us in our turn! When we got close up, every one of them had disappeared, and there was a silence of the grave. We knew that there was something up, but what the move was we could not tell, till from behind the fort came rushing again a fleet of boats. We turned on them, and, like we did before, we made mincemeat of them. This time the tide made for us, and the bobbing heads went by us in dozens. Now and then there was a wild yell, as an alligator pulled some one down into the mud. This went on for a little, and we had beaten them off enough to be able to get our grappling-irons ready for climbing the stockade, when the second lieutenant, who was in the outer boat, called out: 'Back with the boats! Back, quick, the tide is falling!' and with one impulse we began to shove off. Then, in an instant, the place became alive again with the Malays, and they began firing on us so quickly that before we could get out into the whirl of tide there was many a dead man in our boats.

There was no use trying to do any more that day, and after we had done what could be done for the wounded, and patched up our boats, for there was plenty of shot-holes to plug, we pulled back to the ship. The alligators had had a good day, and as we went along, and the mudbanks grew higher and higher with the falling of the tide, we could see them lie out lazily, as if they had been gorged. Aye! And there was enough left for the ground-sharks out in the offing; for the men on board told us that every while on the ebb something would go along, bobbing up and down in the swell, till presently there would be a swift ripple of a fin, and then there was no more pirate.

Well! when we got aboard, the rest was mighty anxious to know what had been done; and when we began, with the heads on spikes of the red stockade, the men ground their teeth, and Old Land's End up, and says he: 'The Red Stockade! We'll not forget the name! It'll be our turn next, and then we'll paint it inside this time.' And so it was that we came to know the place by that name. That night the captain was like a man that would do murder. His face was like steel, and his eyes was as red as flames. He didn't seem to have a thought for any one; and everything he did was as hard as though his heart were brass. He ordered all that was needful to be done for the wounded, but he added to the doctor: 'And, mind you, get them well as soon as you can. We're too short-handed already!'

Up to now, we all had known him treat men as men, but now

he only thought of us as machines for fighting! True enough, he thought the same of himself. Twice that very night he cut up rough in a new way. Of course, the men was talking of the attack, and there was lots of brag and chaff, for all they was so grim earnest, and some of the old fooling went on about blood and tortures. The captain came on deck, and as he walked along, he saw one of the men that didn't like the kreeses, and he didn't evidently like the looks of him, for he turned on his heel and said savagely: 'Send the doctor here!' So the doctor came, and the captain he says to him, cold as ice, and as polite as you please: 'Dr Fairbrother, there is a sick man here! look at his pale face. Something wrong with his liver, I suppose. It's the only thing that makes a seaman's face white when there's fighting ahead. Take him down to sick bay, and do something for him. I'd like to cut the accursed white liver out of him altogether!' and with that he went down to his cabin.

Well if we was hot for fighting before, we was boiling after that, and we all came to know that the next attack on the Red Stockade would be the last, one way or the other! We had to wait two more days before that could come off, for the boats and tackle had to be made ready, and there wasn't going to be any mistakes made this time.

It was just after midnight when we began to get ready. Every man was to his post. The moon was up, and it was lighter nor a London day, and the captain stood by and saw every man to his place, and nothing escaped him. By and by, as No 6 boat was filling, and before the officer in charge of it got in, came the midshipman, young Tempest, and when the captain saw him he called him up and hissed out before all the crew: 'Why are you so white? What's wrong with you, anyway? Is your liver out of order, too?'

True enough, the boy was white, but at the flaming insult the blood rushed to his face and we could see it red in the starlight. Then in another moment it passed away and left him paler than ever, and he said with a gentle voice, though standing as straight as a ramrod: 'I can't help the blood in my face, sir. If I'm a coward because I'm pale, perhaps you are right. But I shall do my duty all the same!' and with that he pulled himself up, touched his cap, and went down into the boat.

Old Land's End was behind me in the boat with him, number five to my six, and he whispered to me through his shut teeth: 'Too rough that! He might have thought a bit that he's only a child. And he came all the same, even if he was afeer'd!'

41

We stole away with muffled oars, and dropped silently into the river on the floodtide. If any man had had any doubts as to whether we was in earnest at other times, he had none then, anyhow. It was a pretty grim time, I tell you, for the most of us felt that whether we won or not this time, there would be many empty hammocks that night in the 'George Ranger', but we meant to win even if we went into the maws of the sharks and crocodiles for it. When we came up close on the flood we lost no time but went slap at the fort. At first, of course, we had crawled up the river in silence, and I think that we took the beggars by surprise, for we was there before the time they expected us. Howsomever, they turned out quick enough and there was soon music on both sides of the stockade. We didn't want to take any chance on the mudbanks this time, so we ran in close under the stockade at once and hooked on. We found that they had repaired the breach we had made the last time. They fought like devils, for they knew that we could beat them hand to hand, if we could once get in, and they sent round the boats to take us on the flank, as they had done each time before. But this time we wasn't to be drawn away from our attack, and we let our boats outside tackle them, while we minded our own business closer home.

It was a long fight and a bloody one. They was sheltered inside, and they knew that time was with them, for when the tide should have fallen, if we hadn't got in we should have our old trouble with the mudbanks all over again. But we knew it, too, and we didn't lose no time. Still, men is only men, after all, and we couldn't fly up over a stockade out of a boat, and them as did get up was sliced about dreadful – they are handy workmen with their kreeses, and no doubt! We was so hot on the job we had on hand that we never took no note of time at all, and all at once we found the boat fixed tight under us.

The tide had fallen and left us on the bank under the Red Stockade, and the best half of the boats was cut off from us. We had some thirty men left, and we knew we had to fight whether we liked it or not. It didn't much matter, anyhow, for we was game to go through with it. The captain, when he seen the state of things, gave his orders to take the boats out into midstream, and shell and shot the fort, whilst we was to do what we could to get in. It was no use trying to bridge over the slobs, for the masts of an old seventy-four wouldn't have done it. We was in a tight place, then, I can tell you, between two fires, for the guns in the boats couldn't fire high enough to clear us every time, without going over the fort altogether, and more than one of our own shots did some of us a harm. The cutter came into the game, and began sending the war-rockets from the tubes. The pirates didn't like that, I tell you, and more betoken, no more did we, for we got as much of them as they did, till the captain saw the harm to us, and bade them cease. But he knew his business, and he kept all the fire of the guns on the one side of the stockade, till he knocked a hole that we could get in by. When this was done, the Malays left the outer wall and went within the fort proper. This gave us some protection, since they couldn't fire right down on us, and our guns kept the boats away that would have taken us from the riverside. But it was hot work, and we began dropping away with stray shots, and with the stinkpots and hand grenades that they kept hurling over the stockade on to us.

So the time came when we found that we must make a dash for the fort, or get picked out, one by one, where we stood. By this time some of our boats was making for the opening, and there seemed less life behind the stockade; some of them was up to some move, and was sheering off to make up some other devilment. Still, they had their guns in the fort, and there was danger to our boats if they tried to cross the opening between the piles. One did, and went down with a hole in her within a minute. So we made a burst inside the stockade, and found ourselves in a narrow place between the two walls of piles. Anyhow, the place was drier, and we felt a relief in getting out of up to our knees in steaming mud. There was no time to lose, and the second lieutenant, Webster by name, told us to try to scale the stockade in front.

It wasn't high, but it was slimy below and greasy above, and do what we would, we couldn't get no nigher. A shot from a pistol wiped out the lieutenant, and for a moment we thought we was without a leader. Young Tempest was with us, silent all the time, with his face as white as a ghost, though he done his best, like the rest of us. Suddenly he called out: 'Here, lads! take and throw me in. I'm light enough to do it, and I know that when I'm in you'll all follow.'

Ne'er a man stirred. Then the lad stamped his foot and called again, and I remember his young, high voice now: 'Seamen to your duty! I command here!'

At the word we all stood at attention, just as if we was at quarters. Then Jack Pring, that we called the Giant, for he was six feet four and as strong as a bullock, spoke out: 'It's no duty, sir, to fling an officer into hell!' The lad looked at him and nodded.

'Volunteers for dangerous duty!' he called, and every man of the crowd stepped out.

'All right, boys!' says he. 'Now take me up and throw me in. We'll get down that flag, anyhow,' and he pointed to the black flag that the pirates flew on the flagstaff in the fort. Then he took the small flag of the float and put it on his breast, and says he: 'This'll suit better.'

'Won't I do, sir?' said Jack, and the lad laughed a laugh that rang again.

'Oh, my eye!' says he, 'has any one got a crane to hoist in the Giant?' The lad told us to catch hold of him, and when Jack hesitated, says he: 'We've always been friends, Jack, and I want you to be one of the last to touch me!' So Jack laid hold of him by one side, and Old Land's End stepped out and took him by the other. The rest of us was, by this time, kicking off our shoes and pulling off our shirts, and getting our knives open in our teeth. The two men gave a great heave together and they sent the boy clean over the top of the stockade. We heard across the river a cheer from our boats, as we began to scramble. There was a pause within the fort for a few seconds, and then we saw the lad swarm up the bamboo flagstaff that swayed under him, and tear down the black flag. He pulled our own flag from his breast and hung it over the top of the post. And he waved his hand and cheered, and the cheer was echoed in thunder across the river. And then a shot fetched him down, and with a wild yell they all went for him, while the cheering from the boats came like a storm.

We never knew quite how we got over that stockade. To this day I can't even imagine how we done it! But when we leaped down, we saw something lying at the foot of the flagstaff all red – and the kreeses was red, too! The devils had done their work! But it was their last, for we came at them with our cutlasses – there was never a sound from the lips of any of us – and we drove them like a hailstorm beats down standing corn! We didn't leave a living thing within the Red Stockade that day, and we wouldn't if there had been a million there!

It was a while before we heard the shouting again, for the boats was coming up the river, now that the fort was ours, and the men had other work for their breath than cheering.

Between us, we made a rare clearance of the pirates' nest that day. We destroyed every boat on the river, and the two ships that we was looking for, and one other that was careened. We tore down and burned every house, and jetty, and stockade in the place, and there was no quarter for them we caught. Some of them got away by a path they knew through the swamp where we couldn't follow them. The sun was getting low when we pulled back to the ship. It would have been a merry enough homecoming, despite our losses – all but for one thing, and that was covered up with a Union Jack in the captain's own boat. Poor lad! when they lifted him on deck, and the men came round to look at him, his face was pale enough now, and, one and all, we felt that it was to make amends, as the captain stooped over and kissed him on the forehead.

'We'll bury him tomorrow,' he said, 'but in blue water, as becomes a gallant seaman.'

At the dawn, next day, he lay on a grating, sewn in his hammock, with the shot at his feet, and the whole crew was mustered, and the chaplain read the service for the dead. Then he spoke a bit about him – how he had done his duty, and was an example to all – and he said how all loved and honoured him. Then the men told off for the duty stood ready to slip the grating and let the gallant boy go plunging down to join the other heroes under the sea; but Old Land's End stepped out and touched his cap to the captain, and asked if he might say a word.

'Say on, my man!' said the captain, and he stood, with his cocked hat in his hand, whilst Old Land's End spoke: 'Mates! ye've heerd what the chaplain said. The boy done his duty, and died like the brave gentleman he was! And we wish he was here now. But, for all that, we can't be sorry for him, or for what he done, though it cost him his life. I had a lad once of my own, and I hoped for him what I never wanted for myself – that he would win fame and honour, and become an admiral of the fleet, as others have done before. But, so help me God! I'd rather see him lying under the flag as we see that brave boy lie now, and know why he was there, than I'd see him in his epaulettes on the quarterdeck of the flagship! He died for his Queen and country, and for the honour of the flag! And what more would you have him do!'

THE HUMAN CHAIR

By *Edogawa Rampo*

Oshiko saw her husband off to his work at the Foreign Office at a little past ten o'clock. Then, now that her time was once again her very own, she shut herself up in the study she shared with her husband to resume work on the story she was to submit for the special summer issue of *K—* magazine.

She was a versatile writer with high literary talent and a smooth-flowing style. Even her husband's popularity as a diplomat was overshadowed by hers as an authoress.

Daily she was overwhelmed with letters from readers praising her works. In fact, this very morning, as soon as she sat down before her desk, she immediately proceeded to glance through the numerous letters which the morning mail had brought. Without exception, in content they all followed the same pattern, but prompted by her deep feminine sense of consideration, she always read through each piece of correspondence addressed to her, whether monotonous or interesting.

Taking the short and simple letters first, she quickly noted their contents. Finally she came to one which was a bulky, manuscript-like sheaf of pages. Although she had not received any advance notice that a manuscript was to be sent her, still it was not uncommon for her to receive the efforts of amateur writers seeking her valuable criticism. In most cases these were long-winded, pointless, and yawn-provoking attempts at writing. Nevertheless, she now opened the envelope in her hand and took out the numerous, closely written sheets.

As she had anticipated, it was a manuscript, carefully bound. But somehow, for some unknown reason, there was neither a title nor a by-line. The manuscript began abruptly:

"Dear Madam: . . ."

Momentarily she reflected. Maybe, after all, it was just a letter. Unconsciously her eyes hurried on to read two or three lines, and then gradually she became absorbed in a strangely gruesome narrative. Her curiosity aroused to the bursting point and spurred on by some unknown magnetic force, she continued to read:

Dear Madam: I do hope you will forgive this presumptuous letter from a complete stranger. What I am about to write, Madam, may shock you no end. However, I am determined to lay bare before you a confession—my own—and to describe in detail the terrible crime I have committed.

For many months I have hidden myself away from the light of civilization, hidden, as it were, like the devil himself. In this whole wide world no one knows of my deeds. However, quite recently a queer change took place in my conscious mind, and I just couldn't bear to keep my secret any longer. I simply had to confess!

All that I have written so far must certainly have awakened only perplexity in your mind. However, I beseech you to bear with me and kindly read my communication to the bitter end, because if you do, you will fully understand the strange workings of my mind and the reason why it is to you in particular that I make this confession.

I am really at a loss as to where to begin, for the facts which I am setting forth are all so grotesquely out of the ordinary. Frankly, words fail me, for human words seem utterly inadequate to sketch all the details. But, nevertheless, I will try to lay bare the events in chronological order, just as they happened.

First let me explain that I am ugly beyond description. Please bear this fact in mind ; otherwise I fear that if and when you do grant my ultimate request and *do* see me, you may be shocked and horrified at the sight of my face—after so many months of unsanitary living. However, I implore you to believe me when I state that, despite the extreme ugliness of my face, within my heart there has always burned a pure and overwhelming passion!

Next, let me explain that I am a humble workman by trade. Had I been born in a well-to-do family, I might have found the power, with money, to ease the torture of my soul brought on by my ugliness. Or perhaps, if I had been endowed by nature with artistic talents, I might again have been able to forget my bestial countenance and seek consolation in music or poetry. But, unblessed with any such talents, and being the unfortunate creature that I am, I had no trade to turn to except that of a humble cabinet-maker. Eventually my specialty became that of making assorted types of chairs.

In this particular line I was fairly successful, to such a degree in fact that I gained the reputation of being able to satisfy any kind of order, no matter how complicated. For this reason, in woodworking circles I came to enjoy the special privilege of accepting only orders for luxury chairs, with complicated requests for unique carvings, new designs for the back-rest and arm-supports, fancy padding for the cushions and seat—all work of a nature which called for skilled hands and patient trial and study, work which an amateur craftsman could hardly undertake.

The reward for all my pains, however, lay in the sheer delight of creating. You may even consider me a braggart when you hear this, but it all seemed to me to be the same type of thrill which a true artist feels upon creating a masterpiece.

As soon as a chair was completed, it was my usual custom to sit on it to see how it felt, and despite the dismal life of one of my humble profession, at such moments I experienced an indescribable thrill. Giving my mind free rein, I used to imagine the types of people who would eventually curl up in the chair, certainly people of nobility, living in palatial residences, with exquisite, priceless paintings hanging on the walls, glittering crystal chandeliers hanging from the ceilings, expensive rugs on the floor, etc.; and one particular chair, which I imagined standing before a mahogany table, gave me the vision of fragrant Western flowers scenting the air with sweet perfume. Enwrapped in these strange visions, I came to feel that I, too, belonged to such settings, and I derived no end of pleasure from imagining myself to be an influential figure in society.

Foolish thoughts such as these kept coming to me in rapid succession. Imagine, Madam, the pathetic figure I made, sitting comfortably in a luxurious chair of my own making and pretending that I was holding hands with the girl of my dreams. As was always the case, however, the noisy chattering of the uncouth women of the neighborhood and the hysterical shrieking, babbling, and wailing of their children quickly dispelled all my beautiful dreams; again grim reality reared its ugly head before my eyes.

Once back to earth I again found myself a miserable creature, a helpless crawling worm! And as for my beloved, that angelic woman, she too vanished like a mist. I cursed myself for my folly! Why, even the dirty women tending babies in the streets did not so much as bother to glance in my direction. Every time I completed a new chair I was haunted by feelings of utter despair. And with the passing of the months, my long-accumulated misery was enough to choke me.

One day I was charged with the task of making a huge, leather-covered armchair, of a type I had never before conceived, for a foreign hotel located in Yokohama. Actually, this particular type of chair was to have been imported from abroad, but through the persuasion of my employer, who admired my skill as a chair-maker, I received the order.

In order to live up to my reputation as a super-craftsman, I began to devote myself seriously to my new assignment. Steadily I became so engrossed in my labors that at times I even skipped food and sleep. Really, it would be no exaggeration to state that the job became my very life, every fiber of the wood I used seemingly linked to my heart and soul.

At last when the chair was completed, I experienced a satisfaction hitherto unknown, for I honestly believed I had achieved a piece of work which immeasurably surpassed all my other creations. As before, I rested the weight of my body on the four legs that supported the chair, first dragging it to a sunny spot on the porch of my workshop. What comfort! What supreme luxury! Not too hard or too soft, the springs seemed to match the cushion with uncanny precision. And as for the leather, what an alluring touch it possessed! This chair not only supported the person who sat in it, but it also seemed to embrace and to hug. Still further, I also noted the perfect reclining angle of the back-support, the delicate puffy swelling of the arm-rests, the perfect symmetry of each of the component parts. Surely, no product could have expressed with greater eloquence the definition of the word "comfort."

I let my body sink deeply into the chair and, caressing the two arm-rests with my hands, gasped with genuine satisfaction and pleasure.

Again my imagination began to play its usual tricks raising strange fancies in my mind. The scene which I imagined now rose before my eyes so vividly that, for a moment, I asked myself if I were not slowly going insane. While in this mental condition, a weird idea suddenly leaped to my mind. Assuredly, it was the whispering of the devil himself. Although it was a sinister idea, it attracted me with a powerful magnetism which I found impossible to resist.

At first, no doubt, the idea found its seed in my secret yearning to keep the chair for myself. Realizing, however, that this was totally out of the question, I next longed to accompany the chair wherever it went. Slowly but steadily, as I continued to nurse this fantastic notion, my mind fell into the grip of an almost terrifying temptation. Imagine, Madam, I really and actually made up my mind to carry out that awful scheme to the end, come what may!

Quickly I took the armchair apart, and then put it together again to suit my weird purposes. As it was a large armchair, with the seat covered right down to the level of the floor, and furthermore, as the back rest and arm-supports were all large in dimensions, I soon contrived to make the cavity inside large enough to accommodate a man without any danger of exposure. Of course, my work was hampered by the large amount of wooden framework and the springs inside, but with my usual skill as a craftsman I remodeled the chair so that the knees could be placed below the seat, the torso and the head inside the back-rest. Seated thus in the cavity, one could remain perfectly concealed.

As this type of craftsmanship came as second nature to me, I also added a few finishing touches, such as improved acoustics to catch outside noises and of course a peep-hole cut out in the leather but absolutely unnoticeable. Furthermore, I also provided storage space for supplies, wherein I placed a few boxes of hardtack and a water bottle. For another of nature's needs I also inserted a large rubber bag, and by the time I finished fitting the interior of the chair with these and other unique facilities, it had become quite a habitable place, but not for longer than two or three days at a stretch.

Completing my weird task, I stripped down to my waist and buried myself inside the chair. Just imagine the strange feeling I experienced, Madam! Really, I felt that I had buried myself in a lonely grave. Upon careful reflection I realized that it was indeed a grave. As soon as I entered the chair I was swallowed up by complete darkness, and to everyone else in the world I no longer existed!

Presently a messenger arrived from the dealer's to take delivery of the armchair, bringing with him a large handcart. My apprentice, the only person with whom I lived, was utterly unaware of what had happened. I saw him talking to the messenger.

While my chair was being loaded onto the handcart, one of the cart-pullers exclaimed: "Good God! This chair certainly is heavy! It must weigh a ton!"

When I heard this, my heart leaped to my mouth. However, as the chair itself was obviously an extraordinarily heavy one, no suspicions were aroused, and before long I could feel the vibration of the rattling handcart being pulled along the streets. Of course, I worried incessantly, but at length, that same afternoon, the armchair in which I was concealed was placed with a thud on the floor of a room in the hotel. Later I discovered that it was not an ordinary room, but the lobby.

Now as you may already have guessed long ago, my key motive in this mad venture was to leave my hole in the chair when the coast was clear, loiter around the hotel, and start stealing. Who would dream that a man was concealed inside a chair? Like a fleeting shadow I could ransack every room at will, and by the time any alarm was sounded, I would be safe and sound inside my sanctuary, holding my breath and observing the ridiculous antics of the people outside looking for me.

Possibly you have heard of the hermit crab that is often found on coastal rocks. Shaped like a large spider, this crab crawls about stealthily and, as soon as it hears footsteps, quickly retreats into an empty shell, from which hiding place, with gruesome, hairy front legs partly exposed, it looks furtively about. I was just like this freak monster-crab. But instead of a shell, I had a better shield—a chair which would conceal me far more effectively.

As you can imagine, my plan was so unique and original, so utterly unexpected, that no one was ever the wiser. Consequently, my adventure was a complete success. On the third day after my arrival at the hotel I discovered that I had already taken in quite a haul.

Imagine the thrill and excitement of being able to rob to my heart's content, not to mention the fun derived from observing the people rushing hither and thither only a few inches away under my very nose, shouting: "The thief went this way!" and: "He went that way!" Unfortunately, I do not have the time to describe all my experiences in detail. Rather, allow me to proceed with my narrative and tell you of a far greater source of weird joy which I managed to discover—in fact, what I am about to relate now is the key point of this letter.

First, however, I must request you to turn your thoughts back to the moment when my chair—and I—were both placed in the lobby of the hotel. As soon as the chair was put on the floor all the various members of the staff took turns testing out the seat. After the novelty wore off they all left the room, and then silence reigned, absolute and complete. However, I could not find the courage to leave my sanctum, for I began to imagine a thousand dangers. For what seemed like ages I kept my ears alerted for the slightest sound. After a while I heard heavy footsteps drawing near, evidently from the direction of the corridor. The next moment the unknown feet must have started to tread on a heavy carpet, for the walking sound died out completely.

Some time later the sound of a man panting, all out of breath, assailed my ears. Before I could anticipate what the next development would be, a large, heavy body like that of a European fell on my knees and seemed to bounce two or three times before settling down. With just a thin layer of leather between the seat of his trousers and my knees, I could almost feel the warmth of his body. As for his broad, muscular shoulders, they rested flatly against my chest, while his two heavy arms were deposited squarely on mine. I could imagine this individual puffing away at his cigar, for the strong aroma came floating to my nostrils.

Just imagine yourself in my queer position, Madam, and reflect for a brief moment on the utterly unnatural state of affairs. As for myself, however, I was utterly frightened, so much so that I crouched in my dark hide-out as if petrified, cold sweat running down my armpits.

Beginning with this individual, several people "sat on my knees" that day, as if they had patiently awaited their turn. No one, however, suspected even for a fleeting moment that the soft "cushion" on which they were sitting was actually human flesh with blood circulating in its veins—confined in a strange world of darkness.

What was it about this mystic hole that fascinated me so? I somehow felt like an animal living in a totally new world. And as for the people who lived in the world outside, I could distinguish them only as people who made weird noises, breathed heavily, talked, rustled their clothes, and possessed soft, round bodies.

Gradually I could begin to distinguish the sitters just by the sense of touch rather than of sight. Those who were fat felt like large jellyfish, while those who were specially thin made me feel that I was supporting a skeleton. Other distinguishing factors consisted of the curve of the spine, the breadth of the shoulder blades, the length of the arms, and the thickness of their thighs as well as the contour of their bottoms. It may seem strange, but I speak nothing but the truth when I say that, although all people may seem alike, there are countless distinguishing traits among all men which can be "seen" merely by the feel of their bodies. In fact, there are just as many differences as in the case of finger-prints or facial contours. This theory, of course, also applies to female bodies.

Usually women are classified in two large categories—the plain and the beautiful. However, in my dark, confined world inside the chair, facial merits or demerits were of secondary importance, being overshadowed by the more meaningful qualities found in the feel of flesh, the sound of the voice, body odor. (Madam, I do hope you will not be offended by the boldness with which I sometimes speak.)

And so, to continue with my narration, there was one girl— the first who ever sat on me—who kindled in my heart a passionate love. Judging solely by her voice, she was European. At the moment, although there was no one else present in the room, her heart must have been filled with happiness, because she was singing with a sweet voice when she came tripping into the room.

Soon I heard her standing immediately in front of my chair, and without giving any warning she suddenly burst into laughter. The very next moment I could hear her flapping her arms like a fish struggling in a net, and then she sat down—on me! For a period of about thirty minutes she continued to sing, moving her body and feet in tempo with her melody.

For me this was quite an unexpected development, for I had always held aloof from all members of the opposite sex because of my ugly face. Now I realized that I was present in the same room with a European girl whom I had never seen, my skin virtually touching hers through a thin layer of leather.

Unaware of my presence, she continued to act with unreserved freedom, doing as she pleased. Inside the chair, I could visualize myself hugging her, kissing her snowy white neck—if only I could remove that layer of leather . . . .

Following this somewhat unhallowed but nevertheless enjoyable experience, I forgot all about my original intentions of committing robbery. Instead, I seemed to be plunging headlong into a new whirlpool of maddening pleasure.

Long I pondered: "Maybe I was destined to enjoy this type of existence." Gradually the truth seemed to dawn on me. For those who were as ugly and as shunned as myself, it was assuredly wiser to enjoy life inside a chair. For in this strange, dark world I could hear and touch all desirable creatures.

Love in a chair! This may seem altogether too fantastic. Only one who has actually experienced it will be able to vouch for the thrills and the joys it provides. Of course, it is a strange sort of love, limited to the senses of touch, hearing, and smell, a love burning in a world of darkness.

Believe it or not, many of the events that take place in this world are beyond full understanding. In the beginning I had intended only to perpetrate a series of robberies, and then flee. Now, however, I became so attached to my "quarters" that I adjusted them more and more to permanent living.

In my nocturnal prowlings I always took the greatest of precautions, watching each step I took, hardly making a sound. Hence there was little danger of being detected. When I recall, however, that I spent several months inside the chair without being discovered even once, it indeed surprises even me.

For the better part of each day I remained inside the chair, sitting like a contortionist with my arms folded and knees bent. As a consequence I felt as if my whole body was paralyzed. Furthermore, as I could never stand up straight, my muscles became taut and inflexible, and gradually I began to crawl instead of walk to the washroom. What a madman I was! Even in the face of all these sufferings I could not persuade myself to abandon my folly and leave that weird world of sensuous pleasure.

In the hotel, although there were several guests who stayed for a month or even two, making the place their home, there was always a constant inflow of new guests, and an equal exodus of the old. As a result I could never manage to enjoy a permanent love. Even now, as I bring back to mind all my "love affairs," I can recall nothing but the touch of warm flesh.

Some of the women possessed the firm bodies of ponies; others seemed to have the slimy bodies of snakes; and still others had bodies composed of nothing but fat, giving them the bounce of a rubber ball. There were also the unusual exceptions who seemed to have bodies made only of sheer muscle, like artistic Greek statues. But notwithstanding the species or types, one and all had a special magnetic allure quite distinctive from the others, and I was perpetually shifting the object of my passions.

At one time, for example, an internationally famous dancer came to Japan and happened to stay at this same hotel. Although she sat in my chair only on one single occasion, the contact of her smooth, soft flesh against my own afforded me a hitherto unknown thrill. So divine was the touch of her body that I felt inspired to a state of positive exaltation. On this occasion, instead of my carnal instincts being aroused, I simply felt like a gifted artist being caressed by the magic wand of a fairy.

Strange, eerie episodes followed in rapid succession. However, as space prohibits, I shall refrain from giving a detailed description of each and every case. Instead, I shall continue to outline the general course of events.

One day, several months following my arrival at the hotel, there suddenly occurred an unexpected change in the shape of my destiny. For some reason the foreign proprietor of the hotel was forced to leave for his homeland, and as a result the management was transferred to Japanese hands.

Originating from this change in proprietorship, a new policy was adopted, calling for a drastic retrenchment in expenditures, abolishment of luxurious fittings, and other steps to increase profits through economy. One of the first results of this new policy was that the management put all the extravagant furnishings of the hotel up for auction. Included in the list of items for sale was my chair.

When I learned of this new development, I immediately felt the greatest of disappointments. Soon, however, a voice inside me advised that I should return to the natural world outside—and spend the tidy sum I had acquired by stealing. I of course realized that I would no longer have to return to my humble life as a craftsman, for actually I was comparatively wealthy. The thought of my new role in society seemed to overcome my disappointment in having to leave the hotel. Also, when I reflected deeply on all the pleasures which I had derived there, I was forced to admit that, although my "love affairs" had been many, they had all been with foreign women and that somehow something had always been lacking.

I then realized fully and deeply that as a Japanese I really craved a lover of my own kind. While I was turning these thoughts over in my mind, my chair—with me still in it—was sent to a furniture store to be sold at an auction. Maybe this time, I told myself, the chair will be purchased by a Japanese home. With my fingers crossed, I decided to be patient and to continue with my existence in the chair a while longer.

Although I suffered for two or three days in my chair while it stood in front of the furniture store, eventually it came up for sale and was promptly purchased. This, fortunately, was because of the excellent workmanship which had gone into its making, and although it was no longer new, it still had a "dignified bearing."

The purchaser was a high-ranking official who lived in Tokyo. When I was being transferred from the furniture store to the man's palatial residence, the bouncing and vibrating of the vehicle almost killed me. I gritted my teeth and bore up bravely, however, comforted by the thought that at last I had been bought by a Japanese.

Inside his house I was placed in a spacious Western-style study. One thing about the room which gave me the greatest of satisfactions was the fact that my chair was meant more for the use of his young and attractive wife than for his own.

Within a month I had come to be with the wife constantly, united with her as one, so to speak. With the exception of the dining and sleeping hours, her soft body was always seated on my knees for the simple reason that she was engaged in a deep-thinking task.

You have no idea how much I loved this lady! She was the first Japanese woman with whom I had ever come into such close contact, and moreover she possessed a wonderfully appealing body. She seemed the answer to all my prayers! Compared with this, all my other "affairs" with the various women in the hotel seemed like childish flirtations, nothing more.

Proof of the mad love which I now cherished for this intellectual lady was found in the fact that I longed to hold her every moment of the time. When she was away, even for a fleeting moment, I waited for her return like a love-crazed Romeo yearning for his Juliet. Such feelings I had never hitherto experienced.

Gradually I came to want to convey my feelings to her . . . somehow. I tried vainly to carry out my purpose, but always encountered a blank wall, for I was absolutely helpless. Oh, how I longed to have her reciprocate my love! Yes, you may consider this the confession of a madman, for I was mad— madly in love with her!

But how could I signal to her? If I revealed myself, the shock of the discovery would immediately prompt her to call her husband and the servants. And that, of course, would be fatal to me, for exposure would not only mean disgrace, but severe punishment for the crimes I had committed.

I therefore decided on another course of action, namely, to add in every way to her comfort and thus awaken in her a natural love for—the chair! As she was a true artist, I somehow felt confident that her natural love of beauty would guide her in the direction I desired. And as for myself, I was willing to find pure contentment in her love even for a material object, for I could find solace in the belief that her delicate feelings of love for even a mere chair were powerful enough to penetrate to the creature that dwelt inside ... which was myself!

In every way I endeavored to make her more comfortable every time she placed her weight on my chair. Whenever she became tired from sitting long in one position on my humble person, I would slowly move my knees and embrace her more warmly, making her more snug. And when she dozed off to sleep I would move my knees, ever so softly, to rock her into a deeper slumber.

Somehow, possibly by a miracle (or was it just my imagination?), this lady now seemed to love my chair deeply, for every time she sat down she acted like a baby falling into a mother's embrace, or a girl surrendering herself into the arms of her lover. And when she moved herself about in the chair, I felt that she was feeling an almost amorous joy. In this way the fire of my love and passion rose into a leaping flame that could never be extinguished, and I finally reached a stage where I simply had to make a strange, bold plea.

Ultimately I began to feel that if she would just look at me, even for a brief passing moment, I could die with the deepest contentment.

No doubt, Madam, by this time, you must certainly have guessed who the object of my mad passion is. To put it explicitly, she happens to be none other than yourself, Madam! Ever since your husband brought the chair from that furniture store I have been suffering excruciating pains because of my mad love and longing for you. I am but a worm ... a loathsome creature.

I have but one request. Could you meet me once, just once? I will ask nothing further of you. I of course do not deserve your sympathy, for I have always been nothing but a villain, unworthy even to touch the soles of your feet. But if you will grant me this one request, just out of compassion, my gratitude will be eternal.

Last night I stole out of your residence to write this confession because, even leaving aside the danger, I did not possess the courage to meet you suddenly face to face, without any warning or preparation.

While you are reading this letter, I will be roaming around

your house with bated breath. If you will agree to my request, please place your handkerchief on the pot of flowers that stands outside your window. At this signal I will open your front door and enter as a humble visitor . . . .

Thus ended the letter.

Even before Yoshiko had read many pages, some premonition of evil had caused her to become deadly pale. Rising unconsciously, she had fled from the study, from *that chair* upon which she had been seated, and had sought sanctuary in one of the Japanese rooms of her house.

For a moment it had been her intention to stop reading and tear up the eerie message ; but somehow, she had read on, with the closely-written sheets laid on a low desk.

Now that she had finished, her premonition was proved correct. That chair on which she had sat from day to day . . . had it really contained a man? If true, what a horrible experience she had unknowingly undergone! A sudden chill came over her, as if ice water had been poured down her back, and the shivers that followed seemed never to stop.

Like one in a trance, she gazed into space. Should she examine the chair? But how could she possibly steel herself for such a horrible ordeal? Even though the chair might now be empty, what about the filthy remains, such as the food and other necessary items which he must have used?

"Madam, a letter for you."

With a start, she looked up and found her maid standing at the doorway with an envelope in her hand.

In a daze, Yoshiko took the envelope and stifled a scream. Horror of horrors! It was another message from the same man! Again her name was written in that same familiar scrawl.

For a long while she hesitated, wondering whether she should open it. At last she mustered up enough courage to break the seal and shakingly took out the pages. This second communication was short and curt, and it contained another breath-taking surprise:

Forgive my boldness in addressing another message to you. To begin with, I merely happen to be one of your ardent admirers. The manuscript which I submitted to you under separate cover was based on pure imagination and my knowledge that you had recently bought *that chair*. It is a sample of my own humble attempts at fictional writing. If you would kindly comment on it, I shall know no greater satisfaction.

For personal reasons I submitted my MS prior to writing this letter of explanation, and I assume you have already read it. How did you find it? If, Madam, you have found it amusing or entertaining in some degree, I shall feel that my literary efforts have not been wasted.

Although I purposely refrained from telling you in the MS, I intend to give my story the title of "The Human Chair."

With all my deepest respects and sincere wishes, I remain,

Cordially yours,

. . . .

LAFCADIO HEARN

Patrick Lafcadio Hearn was born in Lefkada, Greece in 1850. He was baptized in the Greek Orthodox Church, but in his infancy, his family relocated to Dublin, Ireland, where Hearn attended the Roman Catholic Ushaw College. Neither of these religious faiths stuck, however, and when he was nineteen Hearn went to the United States, where he began to work in journalism. He gained employment as a reporter for the *Cincinnati Daily Enquirer* in 1872, and became known as an investigative yet sensational journalist.

In 1877, Hearn left Cincinnati for New Orleans, where he remained for almost a decade. His writings about the city's unique cultural life, especially its Creole population and distinctive cuisine, were published in magazines such as *Harper's Weekly* and *Scribner's Magazine*. His best-known New Orleans works are *Gombo Zhèbes, Little Dictionary of Creole Proverbs in Six Dialects* (1885), *La Cuisine Créole* (1885), and *Chita: A Memory of Last Island*, a novella first published in *Harper's Monthly* in 1888. Over the decade, Hearn became a much-loved chronicler of the city; today, more books have been written about him than any former resident of New Orleans other than Louis Armstrong.

Between 1887 and 1890, Hearn worked as a correspondent in the West Indies, before settling in Japan, a country that would provide his greatest inspiration. At a time when Japan was largely unknown to Westerners, Hearn became world-famous for his writings on the country. His book *Glimpses of*

Unfamiliar Japan (1894) was hugely popular, and in 1896 he began teaching English literature at Tokyo Imperial University. Hearn penned three more books concerned with Japan and Japanese culture. Amongst the best-remembered of these are his collections of Japanese ghost stories and legends, such as *Japanese Fairy Tales* (1898) and *Kwaidan: Stories and Studies of Strange Things* (1903). Kearn died in Tokyo, Japan in 1904, aged 54. His grave is at the Zōshigaya Cemetery in Toshima, Tokyo.

EDOGAWA RAMPO

Hirai Tarō (better known by his pseudonym, Edogawa Rampo) was born in Mie, Japan in 1894. Rampo studied economics at Waseda University, graduating in 1916 and going on to work in a variety of odd jobs. A great admirer of western mystery writers, he modelled his pen-name after Edgar Allen Poe – 'Edogawa Rampo' said very quickly sounds like the American author's name – and began to write his own detective fiction. His literary break came in 1923, when *Shin Seinen* magazine published his story 'The Two-Sen Copper Coin'. It was the first time the magazine had ever published a Japanese author, and the story was popular with readers.

In the following years, Rampo continued to publish stories detailing the committing and solving of crimes. These are notable for their use of codes, symbol systems and meticulous rational processes, and a number of them – 'Case of the Murder on D-Slope' and 'The Stalker in the Attic', for example – are now considered classics of both non-Western mystery fiction and, more generally, early twentieth-century Japanese literature. During the thirties, Rampo turned his attention to stories which played on 'Ero Guro Nansensu' – a Japanese artistic movement of the time – through their focus on eroticism, sexual corruption and decadence. By this time, Rampo was hugely popular in Japan, penning much adolescent fiction that remains highly popular today.

During the Second World War, Rampo's literary output predictably waned, as he and his family moved around Japan avoiding Allied air raids. After the war, Rampo dedicated himself to the promotion and intellectual study of mystery fiction, founding a number of journals. It was during this time that his short stories began to be regularly made into films. Rampo died of a cerebral haemorrhage at the age of 70.

Lightning Source UK Ltd.
Milton Keynes UK
UKHW010631190121
377315UK00001B/209